Dedicated to and inspired by the real Bubba.

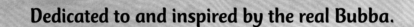

Bubba the Bulldog™
Text copyright © 2014 Bree Clausen
Illustrations copyright © 2014 Bree Clausen

First edition March 2014
Published by Bree Clausen

In his efforts to cheer up his best friend,
Bubba the Bulldog learns that smiling is contagious.

ISBN 978-0-9913871-0-6

www.BubbaTriesToSmile.com

Bubba the Bulldog
Tries to Smile

by Bree Clausen

Ryan laughed around his dog Bubba all the time, but Bubba didn't know why. Seeing Ryan smile made Bubba happy, even though Bubba couldn't smile himself.

When Ryan offered him a treat, saying,

Smile...

                                      Smile...

                                                                  Smile..

he'd lift up Bubba's lips, but Bubba just couldn't hold them up. He always wanted that treat, but his lips were just too heavy.

Bubba's lips were gigantic. They hung down in a
permanent frown. He wished he could smile for Ryan,

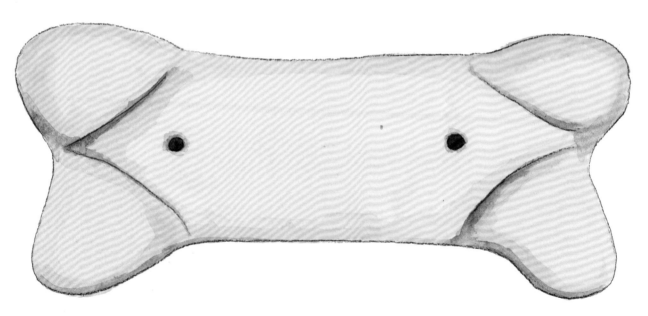

and...

he really wanted that treat.

One day, Bubba leapt in excitement when Ryan brought home a huge bone. He rushed to taste it.

Yuck!
It tasted horrible!

It was so dry that his lip stuck to his gums.

"I broke my leg skateboarding," Ryan cried. Ryan wasn't laughing or smiling anymore. Bubba whined in sadness. He wanted his *happy, laughing* Ryan back.

Bubba brought all his best toys: the squeaky ones, the bouncy ones, even the old stinky ones,

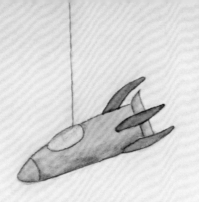

but Ryan wouldn't play.

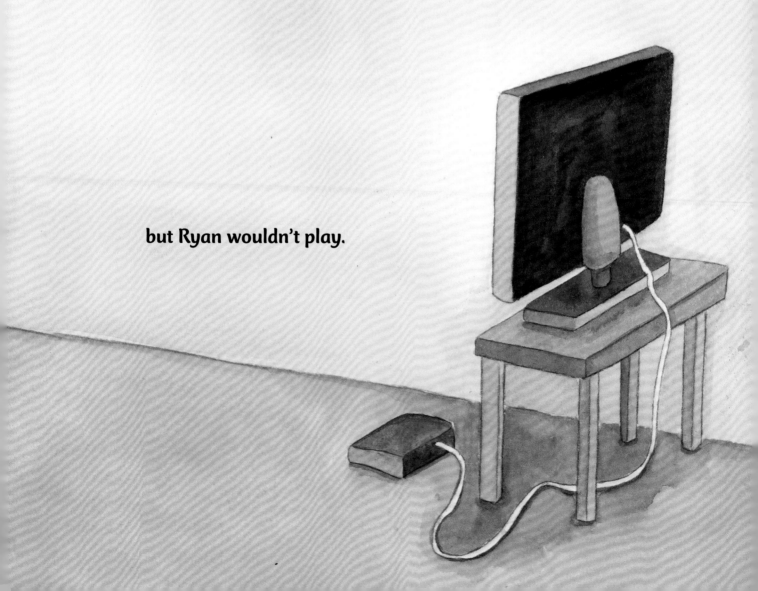

Bubba found a new toy.

He rolled, tumbled, jumped, and pounced around.

Suddenly, he was stuck.

He rubbed his face on the carpet
and rolled around the floor
trying to escape.

The tape
stuck to the dust,
it stuck to the carpet,
it wrapped around his head,
and it even went inside his mouth. It was a mess!

Ryan laughed and said,
"Dude, what happened to you?
I thought I had a bulldog. Now I have a dust bunny! Look! You are
finally smiling! GOOOOOOOOOOOOOOOD boy! You deserve a treat."

Bubba noticed that his lips felt lighter and that Ryan was *smiling* too!
And that made Bubba feel good.

So did the thought of a treat.

It took a while for Ryan to get Bubba clean and to
look like his bulldog-self again.
"You're all clean, round, and I
can see your cute
wrinkles again,"

Ryan said to Bubba
as he gave him a
high five.

That was one trick that Bubba could easily do.

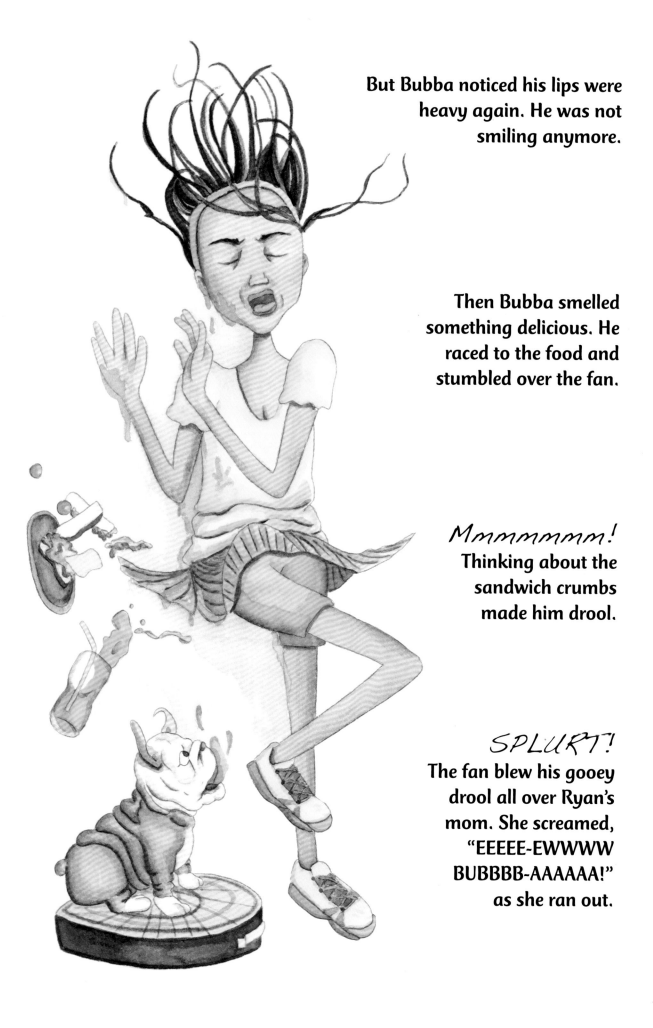

But Bubba noticed his lips were heavy again. He was not smiling anymore.

Then Bubba smelled something delicious. He raced to the food and stumbled over the fan.

Mmmmmmm! Thinking about the sandwich crumbs made him drool.

SPLURT! The fan blew his gooey drool all over Ryan's mom. She screamed, "EEEEE-EWWWW BUBBBB-AAAAAA!" as she ran out.

Ryan exclaimed, "Bubba, you are smiling again! GOOOOOOOOD boy!"

Bubba felt the cool wind under him, making his lips feel lighter, and he saw Ryan was *smiling* again!

That's when Bubba got the idea.

If he could learn the smile trick,
maybe he could make Ryan
happy anytime!

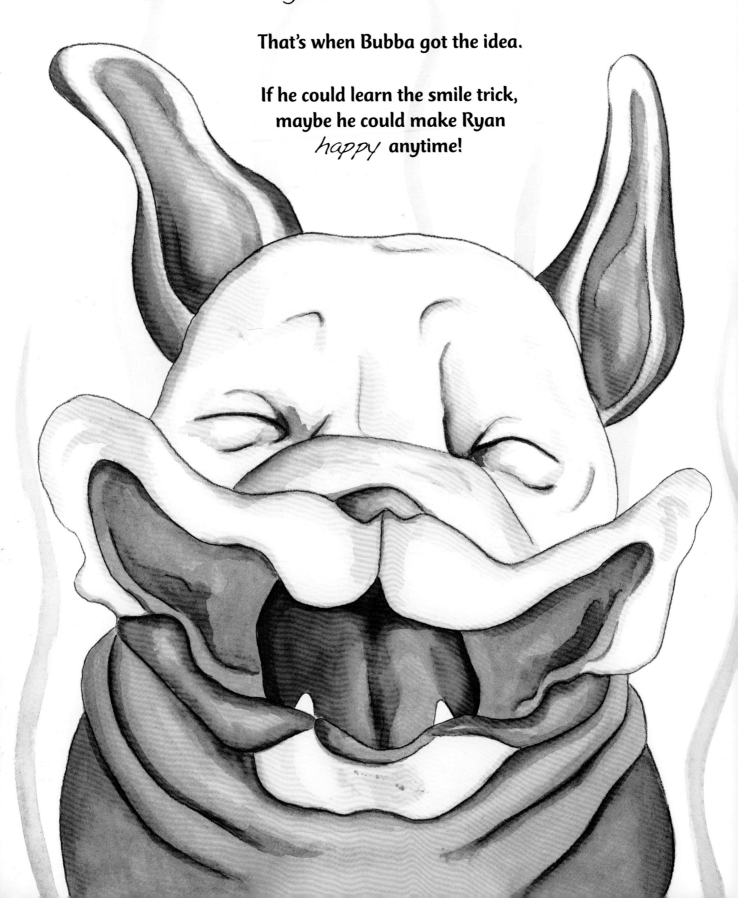

Bubba ran to fetch something to lift his lips. He went to the room that had all the extra stuff. But Ryan said, "Are you sure you want to go into the *BROOM* closet?!"

Oh NO!

Not the

BROOM!

Bubba thought the broom was a scary monster. It was prickly and scratched its long fingers on the floor, *and* it stole all the crumbs off the floor that Bubba wanted to eat!

But Bubba couldn't give up. He wanted to smile for his friend to make him happy again.

Bubba slowly crept into the closet, but his bottom was *bigger* than he thought.

He knocked over the paint,

that oozed onto a baseball,

that rolled into the iron,

that tipped onto a vase,

that hit a hammer,

and kept going until Bubba
turned around and...

SMACK! The broom whacked him right on his behind.

Bubba took off running on the slippery floor. He ran faster than ever before. Unfortunately, he was running in place instead of running away.

He was so scared he almost had a potty accident!

He ran to their room to hide and closed his eyes tightly, but his behind couldn't fit under the bed.

When he opened his scared eyes, he found a world of hidden treasures. And there, right in front of him,

a smile!

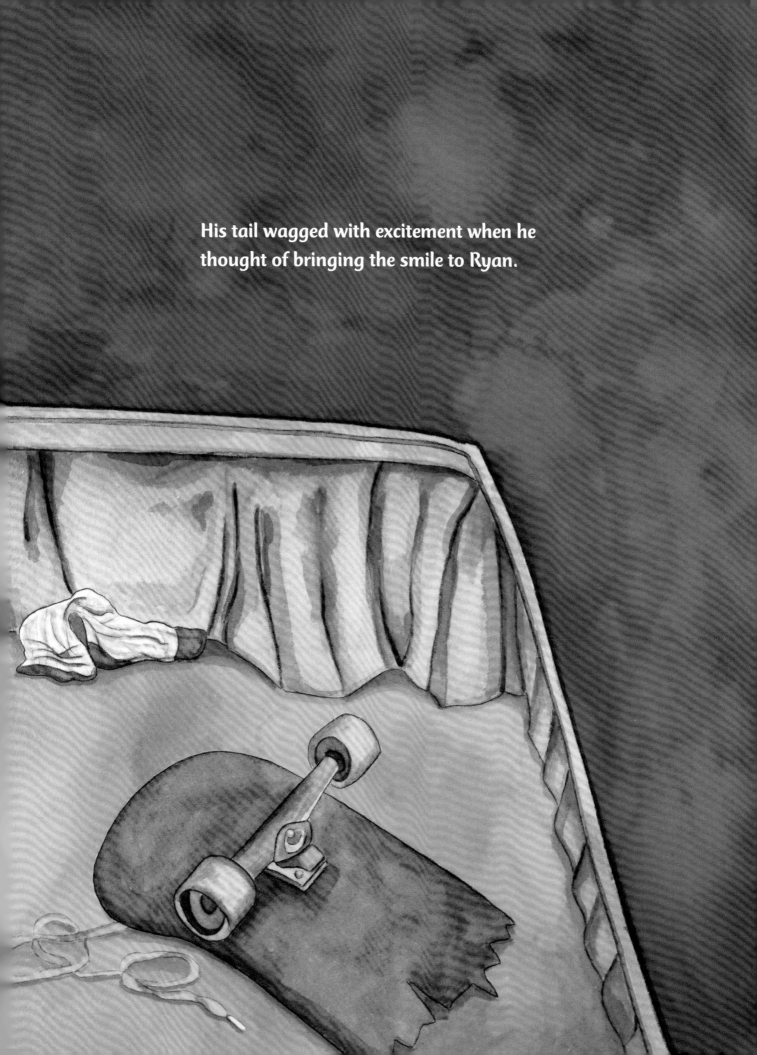

His tail wagged with excitement when he
thought of bringing the smile to Ryan.

Ryan *laughed* and *smiled* the biggest smile Bubba had ever seen.

He kissed Bubba, held him tight, and said, "My leg may be broken, but I'm okay. It makes me so happy to see you smile!"

Ryan hugged Bubba, who let out a loud *THHHTTT!* Once the smell hit Ryan's nose, he laughed and said, "I just noticed something, you little Stink-a-roo. Every time you toot, you smile too!"

Ryan hugged and kissed Bubba, being careful not to squeeze him too tight. His nose couldn't handle any more stinky "*smiles*" for the day.